Mordechai's Moustache and his Wife's Cats

and other stories

D1564505

Mahmoud Shukair

Mordechai's Moustache and his Wife's Cats

and other stories

Translated from Arabic by
Issa J Boullata, Elizabeth Whitehouse,
Elizabeth Winslow and Christina Phillips

 Banipal Books
2007

First published in the UK by Banipal Books, London 2007

A CIP record for this book is available in the British Library
ISBN 978-0-9549666-3-8

The publisher acknowledges financial assistance from
Arts Council England

Banipal Books
P O Box 22300, LONDON W13 8ZQ,
www.banipal.co.uk

Set in Bembo
Printed and bound
by Lightning Source, UK&USA

Mahmoud Shukair has been a prodigious creator of short stories since the mid-1960s. Born in 1941 in Jerusalem and growing up there, he studied at Damascus University and has an MA in Philosophy and Sociology (1965). He worked for many years as a teacher and journalist, was editor-in-chief of a weekly magazine, *Al-Talia'a [The Vanguard]* 1994-96, and then of *Dafatir Thaqafiya [Cultural File]* magazine 1996-2000. He has been jailed twice by the Israeli authorities, for an overall period of nearly two years, and in 1975 was deported to Lebanon. He returned to Jerusalem in 1993 after living in Beirut, Amman and Prague. He has authored 25 books – nine short story collections, 13 books for children, a volume of folktales, a biography of a city, and a travelogue. He has written six series for television, three plays, and countless newspaper and magazine articles. Some of his short stories have been published in French, Spanish, Korean and Chinese, as well as English.

Contents

Shakira's Picture

For the seventh time, my cousin went to line up in the queue at the office door of the Israeli Ministry of Interior in order to renew the document without which he would be unable to travel abroad from the airport. He usually went at six in the morning but was faced with a long queue of people, some of whom had gone there a little after midnight. So he finally resorted to an Israeli non-governmental organisation, whose director took care of the matter once and for all. He was able to make an appointment for my cousin to enter the building, at whose door the people of Jerusalem had been suffering for many years.

This time my cousin arrived at the office of the Ministry of Interior with greater confidence in himself. To tell the truth, he almost lost faith in everything whenever he found himself in a crowd of people impolitely shoving one another. He almost came to blows with two young men who pushed their way ahead of all the other people, including himself. But he decided to avoid trouble and let the two young men do what they wanted. He told no one but me about his suffering because he wanted the people of the neighbourhood to carry on believing he was a man of importance and that no door would be shut in his face.

The guard behind the iron bars of the window shouted: "Talha Shakirat!"

My cousin immediately answered: "Yes, yes! I'm Talha Shakirat."

The guard opened the door to my cousin, who then entered with self-confidence, envied by the crowd that had been waiting for hours. The guard looked at my cousin for a moment, then said: "Shakirat! Do you know Shakira?"

My cousin answered without a moment's hesitation: "Of course. She's one of the girls in our family."

The guard appeared impressed and said: "I'm a fan of hers and I like her songs, do you know that?"

"How would I know that?" my cousin answered: "But I'll give you some of her songs as a present. She sent them to me a few weeks ago." My cousin put out his hand to shake the guard's hand and the guard stretched out his, saying: "I'm Rony."

"And I'm Talha Shakirat," my cousin said. Then he went back down the stairs of the building, feeling happy about this relationship that Shakira's name had facilitated. He was grateful to his grandfather Shakirat, who by coincidence carried this very name, for otherwise Shakira would have been too distant to affect my cousin's destiny and he would then not have had the opportunity of establishing a relationship with one of the Ministry of Interior guards with an unexpected ease he could never have dreamt of. My cousin set his hopes on this relationship for he was in need of the services of the Ministry of Interior's office, and so too were other members of the family. Now my cousin had an aboveboard relationship with a guard (yes, aboveboard – this is a matter my cousin insists on because he does not like anyone saying he has a relationship with the occupation authorities that is suspect); it opened for him the opportunity of exercising his desire to appear as the person able to help relatives and friends who complain about the ill-treatment they are continually subjected to as they wait outside the Ministry of Interior.

My cousin did not waste a minute. As soon as he left the building, he went to the nearest shop selling records and tapes and asked for the latest songs of Shakira. The shop owner sold him several records and my cousin carried them home with extreme care. He listened to them for hours on end, and then he told his father about the fact that one of the girls in the family was a singer. My uncle immediately expressed displeasure at this information because he could not bear that anyone should say anything untoward about the family's reputation. However, my cousin tried to mitigate the effect of this surprise on his father and told him about the guard, Rony, who was a fan of Shakira (my uncle had been trying in vain for months to enter the Ministry of Interior); my cousin also told him about Shakira's success in the world of singing and how the Shakirat family could draw great benefit from such a relationship. When my uncle realized there might be benefits from what he had heard, he perked up and began asking his son for further information about Shakira in order to compare it with his own information about the family tree that he knew by heart.

After some quick examination, my uncle confirmed to the people of the neighbourhood who were sitting in his guest room that Shakira's grandfather was indeed a member of the Shakirat family and that, may God bless his soul, he had differed with his brothers over the division of the inheritance their father had left them. He had chosen to emigrate to Lebanon where he had changed his religion after falling madly in love with a beautiful Lebanese woman who was a Christian and followed the religion of our Lord Jesus, peace be on him; then he married her and had many children, including Shakira's father. If it were not for Shakira's surprising fame in the world of singing, this branch of the Shakirat family would have remained unknown, and no one in our neighbourhood would have had any knowledge of it.

When the whole neighbourhood began exchanging the minutest details about Shakira, my uncle started feeling embarrassed. The girl was portrayed as a loose woman, perhaps because she lived in the western hemisphere of the globe ("In a country called Colombia, my dear sir!" is what my uncle used to say, grumbling somewhat). If the accursed girl had lived here, in this neighbourhood (in our neighbourhood), my uncle would not have permitted her to dance and sing almost naked. My uncle did not believe that Shakira appeared on television almost naked. He did not watch television, but many people told him that they had seen Shakira on the small screen with a bare stomach and with legs shining like diamonds. My uncle listened to their words and did not dare disbelieve them, but changed the subject one way or another and tried to divert their thoughts from dancing and singing to the beautiful past. He spoke of the courage of Shakira's grandfather, how one evening he had come face to face with a hyena in the wilderness but was not afraid of it and was not hypnotised by it. Rather, he fought the hyena until he had killed it, then skinned it and sold it at the lowest price.

When my uncle was all by himself he tended to believe what the people of the neighbourhood had been saying. If they had not seen her dance almost naked, they would not have said that. He used to talk with his son about his misgivings and sometimes cursed Shakira, using harsh words. My cousin did not dare tell his father that Shakira was having a love affair with the son of the Argentinian president. If my uncle knew that perhaps he would have removed Shakira's picture that hung on a wall in his house. The picture had been brought home by my cousin, of course. He found it published in one of the newspapers and had taken it to a photographer and asked him to print an enlargement. The photographer enlarged it and my cousin brought the print home and suggested his father hang it on the wall of the guest room. My uncle thought that was too much and said: "Since when, Talha, have we accepted putting pictures of our women in the guest room, which is frequented by people from all over?"

My cousin cut short the discussion on the matter and hung the picture in one of the rooms of the women of the house. My uncle was obliged to give in to his son. (He was obliged to do that in the hope of help in obtaining a new identity card permitting him to travel across the bridge to Jordan, since he had lost the old one he got from the Israelis when they first occupied Jerusalem.) But he placed a shawl over the picture to hide Shakira's hair and bare shoulders. My uncle did this in order to preserve the good reputation of Shakira and the family from the gossip of the women who came to the house from time to time to visit, and afterwards start rumours.

This was not the only picture of Shakira, as my cousin's office was full of pictures of the young singer. I had observed this whenever I visited him, now and then. I would stretch out my hand to greet him while staring at him with a look that accused him of being a dog; and he would stretch out his hand to greet me while staring at me with a look that accused me of being a jackass. He would say: "You're so old-fashioned. Why don't you move with the times just a little? Things have changed; we now live in the age of the internet and smart bombs!" I would sit in his office that was full of things suggesting modernity. I would follow his continual telephone conversations and try to understand what was happening on the monitor of his computer that sat on his desk. But I learnt nothing, and from time to time he laughed in a loathsome manner, then looked at the monitor. He would make a point of doing that whenever he wanted a rest from talking to me or in order to avoid a question he did not want to answer.

My cousin had many relationships of this kind and was convinced that they would, one day, be of great benefit. For example, when the news spread that Shakira was having a love affair with the son of the Argentinian president, it did not occupy my mind for more than a moment. As for my cousin, he immediately fed it into his web of information for future possible use. "Starting with this bit of news," he said to me, "I'll strengthen my relationship with Argentina. I'll make every effort to become an agent here for some Argentinian companies and one day I may become an honorary consul of Argentina for the whole of the Arab East!" When I smiled derisively, he laughed and mocked me: "You're a simpleton!" (meaning a jackass, of course.)

My cousin has strange ideas. He once challenged me, saying: "I can invite ten men and ten women to my home for lunch. I'll serve them food from empty pots and place it on empty plates for them. They'll eat until they're satisfied and they'll go back to their homes, suffering from indigestion because they've over-eaten!" Bragging of his intellectual powers and assured of his sharp attention to the rhythms of the modern age, and its logic, he would say: "You can create whatever facts you need and at the same time you can persuade a growing number of people of these facts, facts which cannot be touched or whose existence cannot be proved by material evidence! The important thing is that you should have some measure of worldliness, skill and cleverness." For some reason, I used to avoid entering into any such wager with my cousin.

However, my uncle did enter into the wager and he was certain that Rony, the guard, would receive him warmly. My uncle would then tell him about Shakira's grandfather and that, for a long time, this branch of the family was known for loving music and being inclined to singing; and that was why the family was not surprised by Shakira's outstanding talent in dancing and singing. He would relate to him, if his time (that is, Rony's time) permitted, many anecdotes about Shakira's grandfather. My uncle entered into the wager and was certain that he would obtain a new identity card, that he would go to Amman to obtain a [Jordanian] laissez-passer, and that he would then travel to Spain and spend several weeks there. My uncle got used to bragging and saying to others in a manner that aroused their curiosity: "I'm going to go to Spain to visit our daughter!" The people of the neighbourhood knew that all my uncle's daughters lived here, in the neighbourhood, so they immediately asked him: "Who is this daughter of yours?" "Shakira!" he would answer proudly, "She has a magnificent home in Spain where she lives for several months every year."

My uncle would not be content with visiting Shakira ("the wanton woman who has danced to every possible tune!" as he used to say to a chosen few family members), for he decided to go to Hijaz to perform the duty of the Haj, having waited a long time to do that. My uncle never faulted on any prescribed religious duty and prayed the five daily prayers on time every day. However, he felt remorse because in his youth he had committed a few sins. At one time, my uncle had turned his hand to commerce. During the olive oil making season, he used to go to a certain village and buy fifty cans of olive oil; he would take them into a special storeroom he had for this purpose, then bring them out to sell them, their number having become one hundred (he had clever ways of cheating). He used to rub his neck secretly with olive oil, expecting people to ask him to swear that the oil he was selling them was pure oil; so he would pretend to swear, saying: "By my neck, it is pure olive oil!" And they believed him. My uncle divulged this secret to me to mitigate his feeling of guilt, and told me: "I'll go and perform the duty of pilgrimage so that God may forgive me this sin."

My uncle had committed other sins. One morning when the milk woman came to the house he opened the door to her. He liked her tall, elegant body and, without so much as asking, he stretched out his hand to touch her bosom, and started fondling her breast with his fingers. The milk woman pulled back from him, saying, "What a shameless and despicable man you are!" My uncle was embarrassed, and wondered how he would face his Lord in the afterlife and how his condition would be when the two angels, who would uncover his sins as soon as he was buried in the tomb, asked him: "Tell us, why did the milk woman describe you as a despicable man?" My uncle did not tell me of this sin; I heard about it from one of the men of his generation. He insisted he had not committed any other sin, but there are rumours of others.

My uncle entered into the wager despite his great caution. More than once I have heard him express wonder at his son's strong desire to achieve quick fame and wealth. He used to advise him saying, "My son, rega rega![1] Haste is inspired by the Devil." But this time, my uncle threw caution to the wind and entered into the wager. One morning, he went in the company of his son to the Ministry of Interior to get his identity card. I went with them, impelled by curiosity. We went late in the morning because my cousin was confident that Rony, the guard, would jump to receive us as soon as he saw us and that he

[1] Hebrew for 'Slow down!'

would immediately open the main iron door for us. We reached the building and were shocked to see the crowd of people there standing in the heat of the sun. My cousin looked towards the iron grill of the window and proudly said, pointing to a person with long blond hair: "That is Rony." My uncle raised his hand in a gesture of greeting but no one responded. "He's busy. He's always busy with this or that problem," my cousin explained, then added: "We'll wait a little until he becomes aware of us." My uncle asked: "When was the last time you met him?" "Two weeks ago," my cousin replied, "when I brought him a collection of Shakira's songs." My uncle relaxed a little, but a few moments later he seemed to be anxious.

My cousin tried to distinguish himself a little from the people crowding round to the iron grill of the window and at the door of the building. He stood on tiptoe, raised his hand high above his head, and waved to Rony in the hope that he would see him. Rony was busy chiding the people who kept asking him to let them enter the building. My cousin preferred to wait a while before gesturing again to Rony, and was annoyed when he heard my uncle clear his throat to express irritation at the delay. My cousin was obliged to say something so called out: "Rony!" At first he called in a low voice but did not attract Rony's attention. He repeated the call more persistently and with some confidence: "Rony!" Then my cousin called him again, now in a tone mixed with embarrassment: "Mr Rony!" My cousin tried to call upon his own sense of the rhythm and logic of the age, and called out: "Adon Rony! Adon Rony!"[2] Rony looked quickly towards my cousin then for some reason looked away. My cousin repeated his attempt in several languages: "Ma shlomkha[3], Adon Rony? How are you, Mr Rony? Kif halak, ya Sayyid Rony?"[4] It seemed to be clear that Rony heard him but did not pay him any attention.

My uncle could not tolerate the act of ignoring us that Rony, the guard, had put on. He shouted out sharply: "Ya khawaja[5], Rony. Respond to us, Mister!" Rony heard the sharp shout of my uncle and turned to him angrily, demanding: "What do you want? Tell me." My uncle said in a tone full of affection and hope: "My son, Talha, is calling you." "What does your son want? Tell me," Rony said. My cousin smiled in order to ease the tense situation but my uncle had to shoot his last arrow in the hope of refreshing Rony's memory and awakening it from its accursed slumber, so he said: "We are the relatives of Shakira. Eh! Have you forgotten us, my friend?" My cousin seized the opportunity of the silence that ensued and implored: "Permit us to enter, Adon Rony."

Rony answered haughtily: "You have to wait! I'm busy!

---

2 Hebrew for 'Mr'.

3 Hebrew for 'How are you?'

4 Arabic for 'How are you, Mr Rony?'

5 Arabic for 'Mr', mostly used for non-Moslems.

I can't deal with you now!" Indifferent, he turned away. I stared at my cousin: "Dog!" My cousin stared at me: "Jackass!" And we exchanged no further words.

My uncle cut himself off from people for three days, during which he removed Shakira's picture from the wall and threw it violently on the floor. The glass broke into splinters that flew in all directions. My uncle did not travel to Spain, nor did he go to Hijaz to perform the duty of the Haj.

As for my cousin, he told me he would go to Rony, the guard, one more time and take with him a collection of the songs of the daughter of the family, the beloved Shakira – may God keep her!

Ronaldo's Seat

Kadhim Ali paid no attention to the difficulties he was exposed to on account of his enthusiasm for the Brazilian football player Ronaldo. Kadhim Ali loved football but the people of his neighbourhood did not; they did not even have any interest in it. They said: "We have many concerns and have no time to waste on football." His boundless enthusiasm led Kadhim Ali to announce that he was in email contact with Ronaldo. This exchange of emails had resulted in a firm promise from Ronaldo, as Kadhim Ali told the people of his neighbourhood, that the football player and his wife and child would come to visit him and spend a month or two as his guests. Kadhim Ali assured everyone that Ronaldo was indeed coming, no question about that.

So far, there was no problem arising from all this, the people of the neighbourhood were used to hearing strange stories related by Kadhim Ali from time to time, most of which focused on football. After listening to Kadhim Ali, one of them would say to another: "Turn a deaf ear to this story and don't believe what this chatterbox of a driver says." Such words were not said to Kadhim Ali himself directly, but they reached him in one form or another. He was annoyed but continued to give his assurances that Ronaldo was coming.

One morning, one person after another from the neighbourhood tried to sit in the front seat of Kadhim Ali's taxi, but he would not allow anyone to sit in it repeating one sentence for everyone to hear: "This seat is reserved for Ronaldo". The taxi went on its way around the city but Ronaldo was never seen sitting in it, and no one thought of entering into a futile discussion with Kadhim Ali. It was not difficult to pose several quick questions to him: "Kadhim Ali, where's your Brazilian friend?" "Where are his wife and child?" "Where's the guy called Fonaldo?" (Kadhim Ali laughed as he tried in vain to correct the pronunciation of the name.) He did not answer their questions clearly, and this increased the confusion and the eccentricity of the whole situation. He continued to behave oddly and repeat the same words morning and evening – "This seat is reserved for Ronaldo". No one said anything and no one objected, but they did not ask him any more questions.

However, a rumour that no one could have conceived of rose like a storm in the neighbourhood: Kadhim Ali was reserving the front seat of his taxi to make a shameless play for women! One of those living in the neighbourhood had seen him after sunset, the rumour went,

leaning towards a young woman who was sitting beside
him in the front seat – and there was no one else in the
taxi. So Khadhem Ali was a foxy young man, an impu-
dent person using his taxi to serve his frivolous whims!
He should be taught a lesson in morality!

The rumour reached Kadhim Ali but he laughed it off
and said it was the work of someone crazy. The whole
neighbourhood knew Kadhim Ali loved his wife, whom
he married two months after Ronaldo married the young
woman of his dreams. Immediately after his marriage,
Kadhim Ali stopped flirting with girls, contrary to some
other taxi driver friends of his who, though married, did
not give up secret relationships with beautiful young
women. Kadhim Ali held a firm opinion regarding marriage – "Don't marry the young woman you take a first
shine to", although he had been ready to marry his wife
according to this idea. One morning a young woman
had got into his taxi when nobody else was in it but its
driver Kadhim Ali. He had been thunderstruck by her
beauty – and he contemplated her cheeks, her neck, her
fingers. Without any introduction, he said to her: "I seek
to tie the knot with you." The young woman straight
away took off one of her shoes and brandished it in his
face. Had Kadhim Ali not immediately apologised she
would have hit him with it.

For three days running, Kadhim Ali went on a search
for the young woman's house. When he found it, he sent
his mother, his aunt and his sister to make the acquain-

tance of the young woman's family as a prelude to asking for her hand. After several routine procedures, the engagement was effected and then marriage followed. Kadhim Ali continued to be madly attracted to his wife's beauty and he never thought of looking at any other young woman, not even just looking. Now, who was this crazy guy who created a stupid rumour like that? Let this cursed person go to hell!

Yet Kadhim Ali paid the price of the rumour. Three masked men intercepted him and gave him a sound going over. Despite that, he did not stop reserving the front seat of his taxi for Ronaldo. Furthermore, he put up several pictures of his favourite football star on the windows of his taxi. A short time later, another rumour circulated around the neighbourhood: Kadhim Ali was concealing information about someone who had suspicious relations with the Israeli occupation authorities. This rumour spread widely and many believed it, especially after those authorities blew up three new houses in the neighbourhood on the pretext of having been built without a permit from the appropriate government agency. The matter was clear and it did not need much intelligence to understand that the people of the neighbourhood stood in solidarity with one another; not one of them could possibly inform against his neighbour or relative. How could the occupying authorities have known about those three houses? The matter was as clear as sunshine. Suspicions about Kadhim Ali became firmly founded when occupation soldiers made a surprise raid on the neighbourhood one night and arrested fourteen people.

"Actions, Not Words", the movement that had been established a few months earlier and whose members had not exceeded twenty-seven until then, immediately took the initiative. Its leader called the people of the neighbourhood to a meeting, but no more than eight men came to the public square, of whom at least half were members of the movement – and the others were too. The leader of the movement said in a threatening tone: "Let the man called Bonaldo know that we will not condone the deeds of any turncoat bastard, nor will we allow any wanton transgressor to sow the seeds of discord and destruction among us." (The latter threat was addressed, by insinuation, to Kadhim Ali.)

Kadhim Ali paid the price. Seven masked men, unrelated to the earlier three, waylaid him and gave him a sound beating. Despite all this, he continued to reserve the front seat for Ronaldo. Many other rumours circulated because of that, and the future of the neighbourhood became wide open to endless threatening catastrophes. One evening, a man shouted out in the square: "People! Don't we suffer enough from catastrophes at the hands of the occupation authorities without allowing this Kadhim Ali to call down more on us?" A crowd gathered around him and, after some loud arguments, a decision was taken: "We will send a delegation to the family of Kadhim Ali, and his family will have to deal with their recalcitrant son."

Thirteen men, all members of the family, went to the house of Kadhim Ali, led by their elder, the butcher. It was a small house at the edge of the neighbourhood, but it was full of love. Nawal had just finished putting her baby to sleep in his crib and kissed his cheek, saying: "By God, he's the spitting image of Ronaldo's son." Kadhim Ali was happy to hear her remark, which he was hearing for the twentieth time. He went to her, embraced her lovingly, swept her up in his arms, and was lowering her to the ground when he heard violent knocks on the door.

His cousin, the butcher, seized him by his slender arm, pressed against his neck the knife he usually cut the meat with and used to attack his enemies with in the frequent family quarrels, and screamed in his face: "Who is this Konaldo, boy? Talk, say: Who is this Konaldo?" Nawal tried to intervene to protect her husband from the members of his family but she could not. Three of them grabbed her and dragged her to the kitchen, clamping her mouth shut with their rough hands.

His cousin, the butcher, continued to ask in a disapproving tone: "Who is this Konaldo? Tell me. Explain to me." Kadhim Ali kept silent and did not utter a word. He bore the reprimands of his family members, the blows that fell on his face and the sharp edge of the knife that was about to cut his throat. His cousin, the butcher, said: "Listen, boy! I don't want to hear you speak again about this despicable Konaldo, or mention him at all. Do you hear me? As of tomorrow, this Konaldo must leave the neighbourhood, do you understand?" Kadhim Ali did not utter a word but continued to hold in his anger to the end, until the members of his family had left. They gave the people of the neighbourhood a solemn promise that their relative Kadhim Ali would, from then on, cause no problem and that the suspect Konaldo would finally leave the neighbourhood at sunrise the following day.

Kadhim Ali felt humiliated. He cried into his wife's bosom. He wept on her tender bosom. She wiped his salty tears with her lips and spent all night dispelling his worries until his pain subsided and he regained his composure.

In the morning, Kadhim Ali sat behind the driving wheel of his taxi. One of the people of his neighbourhood approached him and was about to get in and sit in the front seat of the taxi. Kadhim Ali stopped him with the decisive words: "This seat is reserved for Ronaldo!"

Mordechai's Moustache and his Wife's Cats

Mordechai was a simple man. There were tens of thousands like him in Tel Aviv. However, he insisted that there were few like him there. He liked to live an easy, comfortable life, not disturbing anyone and not being disturbed by anyone. That was why Mordechai continued to be liked by his neighbours, for he did not disturb them. Mordechai joined the army and left it, but he continued to consider himself a soldier even though he was only a reservist. He practised many trades, simple trades suitable for a simple citizen, but these trades did not yield much money. He worked for many years as a carpenter while Stella worked as a waitress in a restaurant. With the money they both earned, they brought up their son and daughter. Their son became a prominent young man and married the neighbour's daughter, and the couple left to live together in one of the city's suburbs. Their daughter left the family home to live with her boyfriend in a small apartment.

Mordechai was looking forward to living a quiet life

with Stella now that their home was theirs alone. Stella entertained similar feelings to her husband. They were both past fifty now and felt it was their right to live their remaining years in peace and quiet. They prepared themselves for that: Stella kept three cats, two grey and one black with bright eyes, the latter being her favourite because of its unexpected daring and initiative; and Mordechai let his handlebar moustache grow, giving each side free rein to become so long that they covered "the lower sector" of his face (Mordechai was still fond of military terms).

At first Mordechai did not complain about his wife's cats. Rather, he considered them a necessary variation of life that would take its usual course. Stella too did not complain at first about her husband's moustache. She considered it, rather, an extension of the traditions of many soldiers and army generals in Israel and the world who distinguished themselves by their long and thick handlebar moustaches. However, the ends of Mordechai's moustache were unusually long and made Stella complain, and they later filled her with aversion. Mordechai slept beside her in bed and she often woke up in the middle of the night, disturbed because the right end of Mordechai's moustache had settled near her nose. She would be obliged to wake Mordechai so that he could remove his moustache away from her nose. Mordechai would then sleep on his left side, and the right end of his moustache would rise in the air above the bed like a dry, desert plant. But that lasted only for a short while, for Mordechai would not stay long in this position and there would be other occasions for his moustache to toy with Stella's nose before morning dawned.

At dawn Stella's cats jumped onto their bed and stretched their limbs energetically while purring non-stop. Mordechai disliked his wife's cats and complained to her that they did not let him sleep during the most beautiful moments of the morning. Stella did not feel happy at his complaining about her cats and told him he clearly no longer loved the home atmosphere. Mordechai felt his wife had developed a dislike for him or, more precisely, for his moustache, which had become the longest in the neighbourhood and perhaps in all of Tel Aviv. Stella would prepare breakfast and say to him: "Please, come and have breakfast, you and your moustache." Mordechai accepted her words as a sort of pleasant flirtation but, day after day, he increasingly felt sure that she intended to insult his moustache. Despite all this, he would not stop the ends from growing longer, even if they were to become ten metres long.

Mordechai and Stella sat at the table to eat, he and his handlebar moustache on one side and she and her three cats on the opposite side. Stella would look at the moustache stretching out to the right and the left, and say: "It's as if I'm sitting at the airport!" – hinting at Mordechai's moustache stretching out like the wings of an airplane. Mordechai would smile and consider his wife's words a mere joke, but deep down inside he understood them to be nothing but implied insult to his moustache.

Mordechai had sufficient reason to make critical insinuations about his wife, but he avoided that in order not to anger her. He could simply vilify the behaviour of her cats, but he refrained from that out of respect for her. Now the two grey cats were irritating him by rubbing themselves against his legs and making repulsive purring sounds that reduced his appetite more than any time in the past. The black cat then jumped onto the table, not far from the plates of food, and stood there, its body taut and its tail rising upright above its back like a radio aerial. Oh, how Mordechai disliked this scene of the cat's body! It looked as if it was about to broadcast a news bulletin, and Mordechai saw evil omens in news bulletins, so he turned his face away because he could not bear to look at it!

Mordechai stopped eating. He drank his tea as he read the details of the military operation that had taken place in the heart of Tel Aviv the previous evening. After a short while he folded the newspaper.

"I am going to volunteer for military service," he said to his wife out of the blue.

"At this age? They'll not accept you."

"I know people of my age who volunteered to serve at the checkpoints, and they were accepted to go there."

Stella encouraged him to do that because she had noticed his temperament was beginning to get worse as his time spent doing nothing continued. "At least," she told herself, "he will be away from home for some time." Mordechai did not tell her that he was bored with the atmosphere at home. He told her that what had made him take that decision were the positions of Yossi Beilin in particular. He said: "Beilin works against the interest of the state, and we have to defend it against his destructive plans." He said he was angry at the leftist writers who were poisoning the minds of Israelis. He told her he had read an article in *Yediot* newspaper saying that the state would be afflicted with syphilis if it continued to embrace this "occupation".

One day later he put on his military uniform, picked up his M16 rifle, and went to the checkpoint of Qalandiya, south of Ramallah. He stood behind the concrete wall of the checkpoint, a steel helmet on his head. Nothing appeared above the wall except his face, his moustache, and parts of his shoulders and hands. He stared ahead and saw the Palestinians close at hand. For the first time Mordechai stood face to face with Palestinians. He examined their faces and saw that they were silent and anxiously apprehensive as they stood in a long queue in front of the checkpoint, waiting for the opportunity of passing through. He contemplated them. They were a mixture of human beings: men of various ages, old women who could only stand with difficulty, and young women, some of whom wore tight trousers while others were wrapped in flowing garments that covered their bodies and wore white or coloured scarves on their heads. Conflicting ideas and feelings overcame him. He was almost ready to express his sympathy for these unarmed human beings waiting for a hand gesture from him. However, the security of the state was greater than all other considerations and this made him suppress his tender feelings; for these people – in the final analysis – were the enemies of Israel! And in order to strengthen feelings of harshness within him, he rejected any possibility of looking at children, old women, and aged men, and decided to focus his stern looks on young men, the source of danger, the origin of trouble: for it was they who were the saboteurs girding themselves with explosive belts or concealed Kalashnikov machine guns under their jackets to plant death in the chests of Israelis.

Mordechai uttered his first words at a crowd of Palestinians whom he was seeing at close range for the first time in his life, "Fawda mamnu'a![1] Asoor![2] Atem mefinim!"[3]

He heard no clear response from the waiting crowd. He only heard indistinct murmurs and saw grins that made him feel neither comfortable nor at ease. He recognised that being hasty in permitting Palestinians to pass through might cause great harm to the state. At the checkpoint in

---

1 Fawda mamnu'a is Arabic for 'Chaos is forbidden'.
2 Asoor is Hebrew for 'Forbidden'.
3 Atem mefinim is Hebrew for 'You understand'.

front of Mordechai himself, there was – of course – an electronic gate that screened the Palestinians as they passed through it. Opportunities for smuggling arms and explosives were utterly non-existent under these conditions. Yet easy passage across the checkpoint would give an unsuitable impression, for it would appear as though the state were more lax than it ought to be, which would prompt the Palestinians to dare to harm the state and its security.

Mordechai did not want his first day at the checkpoint to have any kind of failure. What would his soldier comrades say about him if even only one suspect were to cross the checkpoint in a moment of inattention on his part? What would Stella say? Despite his meekness, Mordechai was a stern military man when necessary; the past wars in which he had participated, or not participated, were witness to that. Furthermore, who could guarantee to Mordechai that this crowd standing nearby was innocent of any reason for suspicion? If it were up to Mordechai, he would close the checkpoint and tell all those crowding people, whose numbers were increasing every minute: "Lech, lech!⁴ Muroor min hon ma fi!"⁵

But it was not up to him. Yet he had to prevent any attempt by dangerous Palestinians to pass. Mordechai was

---

4 Lech, lech is Hebrew for 'Go, go!'
5 Muroor min hon ma fi is Arabic (Palestinian dialect) for 'There is no passing from here!'

not a god to know what the Palestinians concealed in their hearts. Therefore proceeding patiently and unhurriedly was the best policy in this complex situation. He noticed that a number of men in the queue at the checkpoint were raising their voices, as though they were protesting that he had stopped their movement through the gate.

"Sheket!⁶ Fawda ma biddi!⁷ Atem mefinim!⁸"

The noise increased and many voices were raised. Mordechai exchanged meaningful looks with a soldier standing next to the electronic gate. The soldier immediately closed the checkpoint and the Palestinians were at a loss. Mordechai gave his orders again.

"Uskutu, bitmurru!⁹ Fahmin?!"¹⁰

The Palestinians were divided, some suggesting that everyone be quiet while others vented their anger with further shouts and comments. In the end, the first group had the upper hand. Mordechai seized the opportunity of the closure of the checkpoint to give free rein to his thoughts. He liked to indulge in wool-gathering for it allowed his nerves to rest and gave him an opportunity to contemplate life. At the same time, Mordechai could practise some of his hobbies: smoothing the ends of his

6 Sheket is Hebrew for 'Silence!' or 'Shut up!'
7 Fawda ma biddi! Arabic (Palestinian dialect) for 'I don't want any chaos!'
8 Atem mefinim Hebrew for 'You understand.'
9 Uskutu, bitmurru Arabic (Palestinian dialect) for 'Be silent, you'll pass.'
10 Fahmin Arabic (Palestinian dialect) for 'You understand?!'

moustache with pleasure and enjoyment, and watching women's bodies. He cast direct looks at the bodies of the young women crowding at the checkpoint. He said to himself: "The Palestinians have beautiful girls!" And quickly compared them with the girls of Tel Aviv, thinking: "But the girls in Tel Aviv are more beautiful." It pained him that some of the girls in Tel Aviv behaved immodestly. He once saw an Israeli girl walking in Dizengoff Street and a young man had his arm around her waist. The girl's beauty appealed to him but he was disturbed to see that the young man with his arm around her waist was an Israeli-Arab, heaven forbid! Mordechai attacked the young man and would have killed him had passers-by not intervened to save him. Mordechai did not like to see the girls of Tel Aviv in the laps of young Arab men, the Arabs of the state. That was a bad omen, as he would say, and the state should make a law forbidding Jewish women from marrying Arabs. Mordechai was somewhat sad that the state was remiss in regard to itself, for it ought to make more laws to protect itself from every kind of evil. It ought to make a law about mulukhiya (Jew's mallow) – yes, mulukhiya! The law should provide that cooking it be forbidden except by permission of the army leadership. Mordechai had not yet forgotten that 'joke' which one of the Israeli newspapers quoted from an Arab newspaper made up by a witty Arab. Mordechai insisted that it was not a joke but rather a malicious plan disguised as a joke. The joke went like this:

"There is no need to resist Israel with arms. It is sufficient to gather ten million Arabs along the River Jordan and keep them hungry for the duration of one week. A rumour will then be planted among them that the inhabitants of Tel Aviv are now cooking mulukhiya. They will cross the river immediately, heading towards Tel Aviv. Israel will then oppose and defeat them with its deadly arms and kill five million of them. The rest will be able to remain in the country, take part in the elections of the Knesset, win the majority of seats, and take possession of power in Israel."

Mordechai was disturbed because of that "joke". He believed that the state should be required to observe the borders well whenever the inhabitants of Tel Aviv cooked mulukhiya, and it should be required to observe the borders well, also when the inhabitants of Tel Aviv were satisfied with eating only hamburgers, for it was not yet proven that the Arabs did not like hamburgers! Mordechai woke up from his wool-gathering when an old woman rushed up to the checkpoint shouting: "Are we going to sleep here at the checkpoint? What sort of treatment is this?"

Mordechai asked the woman to go back but she stood firmly where she was. Mordechai's soldier comrade tried to push her back with force but she persisted in shouting and threatening the soldier with her gnarled and veined hands. Mordechai recognised that the old woman had won the round and he had no alternative but to permit her to pass. He gestured to the soldier, and the soldier permitted her to pass. Mordechai then permitted a number of other Palestinians to pass after an inordinately strict examination of their identity cards.

Mordechai felt he needed some rest after all the effort he had exerted. He ordered the Palestinians to wait in the long queue, and he let his thoughts roam freely as he twirled the ends of his moustache. He remembered Stella and felt a flow of vitality run through his loins. He remembered he had not approached her body for three months. He had said he would surprise her this night in a manner she would never expect. He would tell her that military service was indeed life itself and that the army was the living root upon which the state stood. Under the influence of these refreshing thoughts and on account of the dense crowd at the checkpoint, Mordechai permitted a further group of Palestinians to pass. "They say they are a small nation," he thought to himself, "and I bet they are more numerous than the population of China!" The movement of passing through the checkpoint continued at a very slow pace until Mordechai's working hours came to an end and he left the checkpoint and went back home.

Stella received Mordechai with a warm welcome. She listened to his long and often diverging account of the Palestinians whom he had now seen with his own eyes. At times, Stella laughed and pitied the Palestinians; at other times, she felt she hated them. Her feelings were mixed,

31

coloured by the particular events her husband related to her. Then he said to her, as he carried her in his arms to their bedroom: "You will be exposed to some 'heavy bombardment' tonight." He was silent for a moment as he assessed the effect of his words on her, and when he noticed there was no resistance, added: "I will 'advance under cover' of soft light towards you." She appeared to be annoyed and said: "You've gone back to this old jargon. Did we not agree some time ago to forget it?" He asked: "How can you dislike a jargon that titillates feelings?" "I'm not a wall," she answered. "If you want to bombard anything, here is the wall in front of you. Bombard it as you like." Mordechai fell silent.

In the morning, he returned to the checkpoint.

He worked with greater perfection than he did on the first day. He continued to pressure the Palestinians there until they became extremely exasperated. He did not notice until some time later that certain sounds like farting came from them whenever he twiddled the ends of his moustache. At first, he considered it to be a coincidence, something unintended, but the derisive smiles on the faces of the Palestinians and their whispered comments aroused his suspicion. Again and again he shouted, "Sheket, sheket!" "Silence, silence!"

At his order they fell silent. Mordechai seized this opportunity to stroke the ends of his moustache once more and admire the bodies of the beautiful girls, whereupon the farting sounds could be heard again. Mordechai could not exactly locate the spots in the crowd from where these sounds arose, but he was no longer ignorant of their intention as they clearly had no other purpose than to mock his luxuriant handlebar moustache. What should he do? Should he finally close the checkpoint in their faces? That was not possible. There were orders from the higher authorities stipulating that the Palestinians should be permitted to pass. Should he arrest some of those he suspected as the source of these derisive farting sounds, who were mostly a group of uncouth teenagers? Perhaps, but there was no law in the state decreeing that anyone who did that should be arrested. Furthermore, Mordechai did not want to create a scandal on account of his moustache, particularly as the newspapers of the Left might write about the matter and revile both him and his moustache. Yossi Beilin might take advantage of this matter to strengthen his call for abolition of the checkpoints and redeployment of the army from its present positions. Should Mordechai stop twirling the ends of his moustache and thus forego a pleasure he could not give up? This was difficult, very difficult. But it seemed to him that there was no escape from this option if he wanted to preserve the good reputation of his moustache!

Mordechai tried to avoid touching the ends of his moustache as he moved about at the checkpoint. However, the farting sounds did not stop. The very sight of Mordechai's moustache had become sufficient cause for the Palestinians to "play the music" that their lips performed so well. Even Mordechai's colleagues at the checkpoint began to behave in an equivocal way: they defended their colleague's moustache with a wave of scoldings and threats whenever the accursed "performance" started; but, among themselves when they were out of sight of the Palestinians, they laughed with gusto.

Mordechai felt that he was at a decisive crossroads: he should either stop serving at the checkpoint, thus saving his moustache from insults and – at the same time – giving up his sacrifice in the cause of the state; or he should shave off his moustache and preserve his loyalty to the state. (He thought of suggesting that the state should establish an annual award of 50,000 shekels to be given to the ideal citizen, and he was sure he would be the first to receive it.)

And this was indeed what happened: Mordechai decided to shave off his moustache and use this decision to get rid of his wife's cats. Mordechai was confident that she would be obliged, even though it was painful for her, to give up the cats she loved because she so hated his moustache; it would mean she was accepting a kind of exchange between the two of them from which she would both have rest and give rest.

And so Mordechai entered into a long process of dogged negotiation with his wife, which finally ended with success. Stella agreed to get rid of her two grey cats and keep just her black one in exchange for Mordechai's shaving off his handlebar moustache.

And so the next day, Mordechai went to the checkpoint without his moustache.

For their part, the Palestinians noticed that passing through the checkpoint had become a little better, perhaps because Mordechai had given up some of his hobbies and preoccupations!

My Cousin Condoleezza

I don't love my cousin Condoleezza. I don't love her because she's a troublemaker and she has steely eyes that I can't look into. Besides, I am married and my relationship with my wife is as sweet as honey. My mother, Hajja Murjana, wants to find Matheela a husband. She says that if Matheela does not remarry, we must expect a widely publicised scandal. Matheela married my friend Ghattas, who had been a first-year student with me at university. Matheela loved him and he loved her, and thirteen years ago they got married. But their marriage did not last long because Matheela is a shrew whom no husband can tolerate – or this is the impression others have of her. She dumped their son and two daughters on him, then kicked him out of the house, and lived alone, waiting for another chance to marry.

Before marrying Ghattas she loved me, but I did not return her love because I had this aversion to her steely eyes. I did not know who to compare her with until Condoleezza Rice appeared as a famous and influential public figure. I thought: "Eureka! My cousin resembles this woman so much: she has black hair like Condoleezza Rice and is a shrew just like her." I have not told Matheela anything about this resemblance because, if I did, her conceit would grow and one day she would prevail over our neighbourhood, take possession of it by force, appoint herself responsible for it, and impose on us a martial law that might last two or three years.

After her divorce, she created difficulties for us and put pressure on my mother. Unambiguously and unabashedly she continued to express her desire to marry, saying she could not live without a husband. My mother upbraided her for her foolhardiness and blamed her for her perversity.

"You good-for-nothing!" my mother said to her one day. "Since you know you need a husband, why didn't you take care to keep the one you had in the first place?"

"To hell with him!" Matheela said, shrugging her shoulders indifferently. "I could no longer live with him."

My mother lost her patience, and said: "Well! Sit still then, and let me look for a husband for you, every month or so."

This was not my mother's real feeling for Matheela. Rather, she was worried about her niece's foolhardiness, and would like to see her married and virtuous like all the neighbourhood women.

My mother's conversation with Matheela was interrupted only because they became aware of my presence in the next room, from where I could hear everything they were saying. My mother was somewhat embarrassed but not Matheela, who almost ravished me with her glare and said: "The door of my wardrobe is broken. When are you coming to repair it?"

Looking away from her, I replied: "I'll come when I have time."

I left the house, cursing the Israeli occupation that had obliged me and my friend Ghattas to leave university after our first year. Ghattas had become the driver of a Ford taxi and I had become a carpenter after we had both realised that a university degree would not help us earn a livelihood. I used to practise carpentry in my uncle's shop during school holidays. Now it was my turn, so I rented a shop in our neighbourhood and wrote in large letters on its front "Independence Carpentry, owned by Shukri Abd al-Razzaq". In a few years not an insignificant number of people became my clients because − I need not boast − I am a skilful carpenter. For this reason, it seems, my cousin Matheela wanted me to go to her house to repair the broken door of her wardrobe.

I thought to myself: "But I will not go because perhaps she's plotting to ensnare me and make me marry her."

Matheela's ghost followed me day and night and my mother pressured me more than ever before.

I said to her: "What can I tell my wife, mother?"

She said: "What has she to do with that? She should keep quiet and thank God you married her. And don't you forget: a good man marries two or three wives!"

"But I can't," I said, "I can't live under the same roof with Condoleezza Rice."

"Who is this Condeela Imm-Ras?"

"An American woman."

"Good grief! That is the last thing we want!"

My mother does not understand much about politics. She says America's politics is wrong, and when she sees the massacres on TV she says: "The Americans have no mercy in their hearts!" She curses Bush and pours a torrent of abuse on him (but to protect her, I'll not mention any of these words here). She knows no one in America but Bush; she does not know Rumsfeld, Dick Cheney, or Condoleezza Rice; and she does not appear to be happy when I compare my cousin to Condoleezza Rice for she believes Condoleezza Rice must be a miserable woman or else I would not compare my cousin with her.

"Shame on you," she says, "he who makes fun of others will be put to shame in the end!"

I didn't promise my mother anything because I couldn't possibly upset my wife. Yet my wife did feel there was a conspiracy being hatched behind her back and at her expense. She began a campaign against Matheela, initiated by a constant diatribe of information: "Her nose is like a prickly pear; her eyes are those of a female ghoul; her face is the bottom of a bread baking tray." And so on. This was followed by "recalling of ambassadors" and "breaking off diplomatic relations", and expressions like "My head will never talk to hers until death!" Later on, "the borders" were closed, and then "war" began. My wife seized Matheela's hair and twisted it around her arm; Matheela lifted my wife into the air with her strong arms, threw her to the ground, then fell on her savagely; and so the battle flared up! (Unfortunately, neither the UN Security Council nor the Arab League can intervene in such battles!) My wife continued to struggle under Matheela's heavy weight and was about to choke; then she wept like a child, thus announcing her defeat in the battle which Matheela had undeniably won. Matheela stood up and left my wife to deal with her defeat by crying and "beating a disorderly retreat" back home. Matheela went to her home too and waited for me to come and repair the broken door of her wardrobe.

I dreamed of the wardrobe that night. It was there, waiting to be repaired. I was wearing a black wedding suit. My bride entered the room led by her legal guardian. She was wearing a snow-white wedding dress and smiling with hope and desire. Not believing what I saw at first, I rubbed my eyes well to see and recognise my bride's father. It was Rumsfeld, the American Secretary of Defence. He was walking slowly beside the bride. I looked at the bride's face, and saw Condoleezza Rice advancing toward me in the midst of singing and ululations. I was scared because I couldn't bear to be the husband of the National Security Adviser of the USA. This meant that all the world's problems and all the issues relating to fighting terrorism would come from here, and in particular from our home! How could I bear that? I stared at her again and said to myself: "But I married my cousin Matheela!" I went closer to my bride to discover the truth of the matter and, lo and behold, I was face to face with Condoleezza Rice, who took me in her arms and planted a kiss on my forehead. A moment later, I looked around me but saw nobody: neither Rumsfeld, nor my mother, nor anybody else. There was nobody in the room except Condoleezza Rice and me. Condoleezza took off her wedding dress, smiling with a generosity that pleased me.

"It's hot, Mr Shukri," Condoleezza said.

With her naked body, she looked like a nymph.

"Take your time, sweetheart," I said.

(Yes, by God, I dared to say that, was not afraid of an air raid or a Cruise missile!)

"A glass of cold water, please," she said.

I brought her a glass of water in the twinkling of an eye. I followed her movements as she drank the water like a tender gazelle.

I wondered: "Why do people hate America?" And I thought: "I'm now an in-law of the Americans, and whoever curses the Americans in my presence will hear me curse all his forefathers from first to last!" (I will ask my mother not to badmouth my Uncle Dubya, George W. Bush; otherwise, there will be a fight between us.)

My sweetheart walked around the room thinking of

something. I walked behind her as though I were her shadow. I remained silent in case I interrupted her train of thought. I said to myself: "In a short while, my sweetheart will be lying on the bed and I will lie beside her, and this night will be one of the most beautiful of my life."

But Condoleezza continued to walk around the room for a long time, lost in deep thought to such an extent that she was no longer aware of my existence. I thought: "It's clear, Condoleezza is miffed because (stupid that I am) I have not taken off my clothes; and she considers this a sort of insult that can't be tolerated. I should have taken off my clothes the same moment she did so that there would be a perfect scene and complete harmony." So I took off my clothes and stood before her like an infatuated lover.

"Come to bed, sweetheart," I said tenderly.

"Now? This very moment?"

"Is there anything on your mind taking you away from me, Condo?"

"Can't you wait?"

"How long? Ten minutes? Half an hour?"

"Oh, my God! You have to wait until we finish the great Middle East project."

"How long will finishing this project take?"

"Two or three years. We may have to start a war or two."

"What after that, sweetheart?"

"Whole nations will enjoy democracy as a result! You and I will then rejoice."

"But what kind of democracy will this be, Condo, if it is imposed by force, I mean? Is this reasonable?"

"Shut up! Be still, be quiet!"

She seized me by the arm and led me to the door.

I woke up, suffering, my mouth completely dry. I got out of bed and went to the kitchen. I drank a glass of water and remembered Matheela. I said: "I'll find a solution to her problem. She's my cousin, and it's not right for me to spurn her."

In a moment of clear thinking I blamed myself, because I had accused her of being harsh. I said to myself: "She's a poor woman, just perhaps a little more sensuous than is usual." I said: "She's a human being who has her own particular feelings and we must respect these feelings, after all." For a reason I didn't know, my heart became tender towards her that night, perhaps because in my sleep I had seen her exciting body. (Did I see her body or Condoleezza Rice's?) I said: "I'll put an end to my mother's persistence and find a solution to Matheela's problem. I'll begin with my friend Ghattas: I'll try and convince him to return to Matheela and I'll persuade Matheela to return to her husband."

I was not building my plan on illusions, for my mother had said Matheela accepted the idea of returning to her husband after experiencing the difficulty of living alone. Furthermore, there was a problem that weighed equally heavily on Ghattas and Matheela, namely, the fate of the children and the burden of bringing them up. This was a problem that would help bring them together again.

I went to Ghattas, whose news I no longer knew much about since the time we both left the university. I discovered by coincidence that after divorcing Matheela he had gone a long way down the road of vagrancy, or more correctly, a long time before. (Perhaps this was the cause of their divorce but Matheela did not want to expose him.) He frequented Israeli prostitutes, associated himself with them, and spent a long time with them. (During his university studies Ghattas was a member of one of Palestinian resistance organisations and I was a member of the Party. After being imprisoned for five years, he left the organisation because he was afraid and was no longer able to endure the pains he suffered, although he continued to envy the courage of his colleagues who continued their resistance. I left the Party after the demise of the Soviet Union. My morale collapsed but I did not renounce my convictions. I kept "going straight",' as I liked to claim.) Finally, Ghattas came to know a Russian young woman, whose beauty, soft body and fair complexion were captivating. She said she had a Jewish grandmother, who she used to live with in Moscow, and that she had emigrated to Jerusalem in order to practise what she considered to be her natural right of return to the Promised Land. (This is the right that the Palestinian refugees, uprooted from their own country, are deprived of.) Ghattas got to know her and fell in love with her; he said to me he could no longer think of returning to Matheela. "Matheela," he said, "was part of the past. Svetlana is the present." (Svetlana left him after less than a year.) I said to him: "You have disappointed me!" and I went away.

* * *

One evening Matheela had put on a new dress and was waiting for me to come and repair the broken door of her wardrobe.

After some hesitation I went to her.

VIGNETTES

A Spear

As we were leaving our room on the eleventh floor and going to the lift, she said: "Where are you going, carrying that spear with you?" I knew I could not make it fit in the lift, so I stood perplexed like a stupid person but did not suggest that we use the stairs. "Leave it here," she said, "the city's safe and you won't need it." So I left the spear near the lift door, although I did not like the idea. We went down and out of the hotel and walked in the city's crowded streets. One of the hotel servants caught up with me and said, panting: "This is your spear. I found it near the lift door." I took it, and continued walking with my companion. People around us took off their hats in respect to us, thinking perhaps that we had just arrived from the fifteenth century.

A Restaurant

He spent a whole night in the room of the young woman who worked as a waitress in a restaurant.

He lay beside her, but could not sleep because of the food smells coming from her dress that was hanging over the bed-end, and the words her lips continued to utter while she slept, as though she were still at the restaurant running among the customers carrying dishes of food.

Later he spoke to his friends about this young woman of indescribable innocence, whose dreams were all about mezze and main courses, bowls of fruit and after-dinner coffee. As for her, because of her daily preoccupations she did not remember to even mention him to her female friends; after five hours of a work day full of strenuous toil, she had quite forgotten about him.

A Piece of Cloth

They arrived in a city known for its quietness. People there were peaceful and did not come to blows in the streets. Life went on quietly and there were no military vehicles at all in the city. They chose a restaurant with tables on the pavement. There was a gentle breeze caressing faces and women's hair. They chose a table for dinner next to a tall tree: the man chose the side opposite the trunk and the woman the side beside the trunk. The night breeze wafted playfully over her hair as though it were its spoiled child.

She looked around her and seemed to feel everything was fine, so she sat down; but as she moved the chair slightly, one of the legs sank into the square bed surrounding the trunk of the tree. She lost her balance and toppled to the ground. Blood flowed from her forehead and drenched the locks of hair dangling over her eyes.

An ambulance arrived. After midnight, a car took her back to the hotel. She entered the room, the man circling her waist with his arm lest another unexpected surprise should happen.

She took off her clothes, and was stark naked except for a piece of white cloth covering her forehead. She examined the legs of the bed, then lay down and fell into a deep sleep as the man lay beside her, guarding her from any mishap, expected or unexpected.

Meekness

I loved her because she was an actress. Whenever I saw her on stage playing the role of Dolethenia, I said to myself: "Here, I am losing her for ever. She's not the woman I know, or that's what I imagine." But every time she took off her acting clothes and we went back to our room at the hotel, I would get to know her again as she snuggled in my lap like a baby, or like a meek dove that has no thoughts, even in dreams, of the hunter, or of bullets that penetrate the heart.

A Shroud

One evening she went to the city.

She paid no attention to the street lights or to the men on the pavements. She paid attention to nothing, because she was unconscious.

She went to the city in an ambulance, two days after giving birth to her baby who had died after a few hours. The doctors placed the stethoscope under her breast to listen to the beat of her heart. Her breast was full of the milk the baby would never suck. They tightened a band round her arm and measured her blood pressure. Her arm was sad because it would never hold the baby. A nurse came to her and gave her an injection in her belly, just below her navel. Her belly remembered it had said a tender goodbye to the baby when it left.

Three days later, neither her breast nor her arm nor her belly had any more words. She returned from the city in a shroud.

A Loss

She walked beside him as they crossed the main street of the village. He was exhausted and afraid. She said to him: "Sit here. I'll go to the fountain and bring some water." She went away to bring water – and here was the start of her being mistaken. Did she have to go to the fountain on her own? But, what is the meaning of this question? Were the murderers right to do what they did? When she returned from the fountain, she did not find him in the place she had left him. She looked for him for a long time; meanwhile, he was drowning in his own blood at the foot of the mountain.

A Shop

One spring morning, a woman entered the square parallel to Cordoba's main market and headed for the shop of Abu Ahmad al-Qortobi who sold women the most magnificent kinds of material.

She stood in the shop doorway and said something to Abu Ahmad. Nobody in the market heard any of her words, but they observed in his eyes a look of being swept away. The woman left and returned to where she had come from. Abu Ahmad al-Qortobi closed his shop and walked off in her direction.

The people of the market expected that he would return in two or three hours; but he did not. His shop has been closed since the thirteenth century and no one has re-opened it.

Farewell

He walked to her home without thinking of the consequences. He was led to it by his five senses. She was surprised to see him standing at her door. She was wearing a rose-coloured apron that covered her bosom and stomach, and in her hand held a kitchen knife with which she was peeling an onion.

He said: "I've come to bid you farewell, for we shall not meet again after this moment."

"You've come at an inconvenient time," she said. "I smell of onions and my son will soon be returning from school."

She apologised and closed the door. He went away, not knowing when it might be convenient to go back. He hesitated, then changed his mind and turned back – his desire to be decisive was resolute.

At the door, he found a woman who had come to bid her friend farewell. The woman opened the door for the second time in five minutes and embraced her friend, not minding the smell of onions, but did not greet him because she had already done that a few minutes earlier. She said: "I'm expecting my son to return from school in a short while." (She did not know the school was besieged by soldiers.) Then she closed the door.

The man and the woman went off in the same direction and it seemed they wanted to walk together a little longer. They parted company after half an hour, feeling that the moment of farewell had not yet come.

Mosaics

I returned to the city after a long absence. I walked through the streets I had known before, but neither the streets nor the pavements recognised me. I moved from one café to another and from one restaurant to another. There were beautiful waitresses who had come from neighbouring countries looking for work. They looked suspiciously at almost everything because they knew that the owners of cafés and restaurants would not pay them severance when they let them go. Unfortunately, neither the cafés nor the restaurants nor the waitresses recognised me.

A tableau on the wall inside the Golden Well Restaurant was the only thing that I recognised and was recognised by. It consisted of compact, tiny pieces of mosaics forming a scene inspired by The One Thousand and One Nights in which the dignified sultan sat on a soft seat and a slave girl stood before him offering him a drink, while a friendly dog lay near his right foot.

I was later absent from the city for fifteen years, and after this absence returned to see how it had changed. There were many books in a variety of languages now; there were newspapers and internet cafés that had not been there before; there were casinos, Mafia gangs, huge commercial buildings of the American type that had not been there before. Everything had changed. The tableau that I recognised and was recognised by had also seen some change, or that is what I believed: the sultan was still sitting, as I had known him, on his soft seat, and the slave girl was still standing in front of him offering him a drink; but the dog had moved a little from its former place and was nearer the sultan's foot.

Breakfast

While I was in the little restaurant of the boarding-house, I could not help noticing the woman tourist who appeared to have entered middle-age without any anxieties, perhaps because she still retained some elegance and perhaps because she had big hips and an extremely thin husband, who appeared as though he was about to wilt or break.

They entered the restaurant, she first and he behind, following her obediently. His hesitant walk made him appear like a spoiled child led forcibly by his mother to the dining table. They entered and we exchanged greetings as I drank my lemon juice. I followed the curves of the woman's body with my eyes as she moved about, going and coming, toasting slices of bread, putting cheese on her plate as well as mortadella, butter and jam. Meanwhile, her husband looked at the buffet and did not appear to be interested in taking any of the food on offer. He was content with a cup of tea and sat on the edge of his chair like a bird, whereas his wife's hips overflowed beyond the edges of her chair. She ate her food with visible pleasure and, from time to time, exchanged tender words with her husband; then she rose to fetch some cheese, mortadella, cucumbers and a banana for him. He hesitated for some time then ate without appetite, muttering some inaudible words and then suddenly smiling before returning to his silence again. In the meantime, the woman seemed to be fully in tune with the place.

I finished eating my breakfast and stood up to go. Before I left, I joyfully said to them: "Bon appétit!" Then I walked away.

The Department Store

I went to the department store to buy a knife and an orange squeezer. The doctor had advised me to drink orange juice wherever I went so as to prevent a stroke from a blood clot on the brain, which could happen at any moment. I left the boarding-house and headed for the department store. I looked at the five-storey commercial building and could not believe I had ever been there before. But it was here that I had bought my black overcoat which looked like the ones policemen wear; it had accompanied me on many trips and I got rid of it only three years ago. It was here that I had bought shirts and ties at a time when having a stroke would never have occurred to me.

I wandered around the store a little and remembered snippets of my life that had happened here. Then I went to the department where I could buy a knife and an orange squeezer. There were no customers in that department, and I thought: "This is better for me, I will be spared the waiting." The saleswoman, who was forty or a little older, was speaking brusquely into her cell phone. I left her alone and chose a knife that looked like a little dagger. Then I chose a plastic orange squeezer and headed for the cash counter where the saleswoman was standing, still engaged in a sharp conversation on her cell phone. I contemplated her and waited. I did not want to interrupt her conversation. I gestured to her to take her time for I was ready to wait.

I had to wait longer than I had anticipated as, while she was speaking on the phone, she suddenly fainted and fell to the ground. I had to call an ambulance and give a statement to the police. I did not return to my boarding-house until several hours later – with the knife and the orange squeezer.

A Dog

I saw him standing near King Karl Bridge. I approached him and said: "I think I know you!" He said: "Yes, Sir. I'm not surprised about that." Then he asked: "Are you a detective?" I replied: "No. I'm a mere reader of books." Then I asked: "Are you waiting for anyone?" "Yes," he answered, "I'm waiting for a woman and her dog." Then he added: "I'm going to steal the dog, sell it, and with the proceeds buy some wine." "You've never been a thief," I said, "what's happened to you?" He ignored my question and continued: "I've brought a piece of meat with me! When the dog smells the meat, it'll follow me; I'll walk away and it'll follow me."

I saw him scrutinise the crowds of passers-by crossing the bridge. "Here she comes," he suddenly said. "I've been observing her for three days. Her dog walks behind her and she never turns around to look at it because she is sure that it follows her like her own shadow."

Then I saw him clap his hands together in distress. He exclaimed: "Do you see that! The dog's not following her." I said: "Perhaps she left it at home." "Impossible," he said, "someone else must have stolen it!"

I saw him rack his brains and a look of stupidity came over his face. He said: "This lady cannot live without a dog following her." Then he added: "Will you bet on that?" I said: "I don't bet." He commented: "You don't bet and you're satisfied with wasting my time." Then he said: "I'm going to follow the lady now!" He repeated: "I'm going to follow the lady."

I watched him walk off, and I left.

A Pavement

She lay in broad daylight on the pavement under a tree. The street was in a quiet neighbourhood, where elegant cars pass through from time to time. The girl lay in the shade of the tree under a cover hardly enough to cover her body. A bare leg was visible at the lower edge of the cover and her left breast was exposed as though it intended to peek out at the street to enjoy the sight of cars passing by, not paying attention to any one. The girl had no home, and this pavement was the only solution she had to her problem.

A woman invited her to her home in the city. She made
her go into the bathroom, and told her to take off her tat-
tered dress, and her knickers that were infested with lice
and fleas. She brought her a clean dress and knickers, and
left her in the warm water for twenty minutes.

She grilled some fish on the fire for her, and poured her
a glass of wine. The girl ate the fish with great appetite
and drank the glass of wine. The woman offered her a cigarette, but the girl did not take it, saying she had not
learned that disgusting habit. The woman let the girl's
blunt words pass, smiling a smile that could be given more
than one interpretation, and said to her: "In an hour, a
wealthy nobleman will come, and you must be pleasant to
him."

Not a flicker crossed the girl's face. She sat, waiting.
When the woman went to the bathroom, the girl sneaked
away and went immediately back to the pavement.

Supper

I saw him eating supper at the summer restaurant near the
statue of the monk, Jan Haus, and there was a young
woman with him. He was engrossed in gobbling fish
while she ate slowly, as though she feared he would
rebuke her if she imitated him in gobbling up her food. I
expected him to look, by coincidence, towards me and to
know that I was the one who had met him at the bridge
in the morning. But he did not look in my direction,
maybe because he was engrossed in eating and in telling
stories. He would gobble a morsel and swallow it, take a
gulp of his wine, then tell a story; he would interrupt his
story-telling to gobble more food, and then continue.
Meanwhile, the young woman listened to him with
interest and, from time to time, took her share of food –
but in moderation.

He said to her: "I have never led a vagabond life,
tramping the streets." He added: "I've always had a home
to live in. I've lived in several homes in this city, homes
owned by respectable women. They tolerated me if I did

not pay them the rent on time. Though, sometimes they were angry with me when I did not pay them anything for many years."

I noticed that the young woman appeared to have a high regard for him (or she was pretending). He said: "You can live at home with me if you like. Tomorrow I'll buy you a dog, bring it home and dye its fur a suitable colour. You'll be able to go for a walk on King Karl Bridge and take the dog with you. But I must tell you now – 'Beware of thieves'."

I saw her get up and say she would come back in a short while. He followed her with his eyes for a moment, then returned to gobbling his food. He happened to turn around and saw me. He smiled stupidly but said nothing. The young woman did not come back to him because, it seems, she was afraid of his inordinate desire to tell stories.

Mahmoud Shukair

A Home

I saw him on Saladin Street. He was standing near a shop selling gold jewellery and had a stupid smile on his innocent face. I asked him: "Why have you come here?" He said: "Are you from this city?" I asked him: "Are you in any doubt about that?" He did not answer my question. I asked: "Do you remember we met earlier?" He answered: "I'm not sure, perhaps." I asked: "But why have you come here?" He said: "To escape the First World War!" I said: "That war ended a long time ago." He said: "As far as I'm concerned, that war hasn't ended." I said: "Peace is still far from this land!" He said: "I thought it was near; that's why I've come here." I asked: "Do you still steal dogs?" He asked: "Are you a detective?" I said: "Have you forgotten me? Have you forgotten that lady you followed near the bridge?" He said: "Now I remember! She thought I was her dog because I followed her like her own shadow!" I asked: "What did you do to make her think you were her dog?" He said: "I barked behind her until we reached her home." "And then?" I asked. He

66

said: "I let her go to sleep, stole what was equivalent to the price of ten dogs from the house, and then left."

I then watched him walk off, and I left.

Water

The clouds moved across the sky and the drizzle stopped. The fifty-year-old woman left her room on the third floor and went down to the entrance hall wearing a light dress and high-heeled shoes, and carrying an umbrella under her arm.

In the hall, she saw the boarding-house caretaker and her child who was shut up outside in a parked car. She also saw a sixty-year-old man who was staring at her dress with curiosity. Her body quivered for the first time in a year. The caretaker said to her: "The rain has stopped." She said: "Yes, I've seen that from the window of my room, and so now I'm going out." The man said, without introduction: "You're wearing a light dress and going out! It may start raining again." She said: "I have my umbrella." (She noticed his unaffected style of talking, like her husband who had died a year before from bone cancer.) He continued: "Be careful your heels don't get

caught in the narrow cracks between the pavement slabs!"
She laughed, remembering her husband who used to
warn her about this repeatedly whenever she was about to
go out. She did not explain why she laughed: she was
spared that by the innocent laugh that the boarding-house
caretaker was so kind to join in with.

Finally, the woman had to take her leave, because
remaining a prisoner in the hall was not pleasant. She
walked daintily because she did not want to trip on the
pavement and get her light dress wet from the rainwater.

Sorrow

In the dark he looked at his wrist watch. She looked at
her wrist watch too. She said: "We'll not wait a minute
longer. We have to go at once. Sorrow knows the way
very well."

Seduction

They went to the sea on foot. She had said: "We'll take the bus to the sea." And he had said: "We'll walk, and benefit from the exercise." She had not objected, but harboured some hatred toward him. Half way there she said she felt tired. He did not take kindly to this hostility but held his peace. They waited until the bus came.

She said a small bottle of sea water would be enough for her because she did not like carrying a heavy suitcase back home. He said he shared that opinion. She said: "A little sea water is good for one's complexion." He said he was not an expert in that regard but would accompany her to the sea so that she could fill the bottle she had brought with her from the hotel. She noticed that he commented on her words with a certain coolness, and harboured another charge of hatred toward him.

When they reached the seashore, she said she was afraid her shoes would get wet, so suggested that he take off his shoes and walk in the water. He said: "I'll do it in my own way." He took the bottle and went off. She sat waiting for him, recalling Dolethenia whose lover had been absent from her in faraway places. He moved a short distance away from her. He gestured to a young woman swimming near the shore and threw the bottle to her. The young woman filled it with water and walked out of the sea toward him with the water dripping from her seductive body.

He returned to her slowly. She contemplated him for a moment, then said how she hated him and now understood how far apart they were from each other!

A Meeting

After meeting several times, she became attached to him. She said she was no longer able to live without him. He left her, saying: "This is our last meeting." She said, as she painted her toenails with crimson nail polish: "That's what you said last time."

Wind

We were three friends, walking under the autumn rain, when the only umbrella with us broke as we were on the road leading to the church that tourists visited. Our friend said he always liked to have an umbrella of the old kind so that he could lean on it when there was no rain. The wind wrenched apart the metal spokes of the umbrella and turned the fabric inside out in a pitiable manner. We made it an opportunity for a joke, then hastened to the nearest café because the church was still a way off.

We drank tea in the café while the wind battered the trees in the neighbourhood and the rain continued to splosh and splatter like a grumpy, difficult child. Meanwhile, we carried on with our jokes and chats about the broken umbrella.

At the height of our talk, I took hold of the umbrella and tried to return it to its former shape. It resisted and would not comply. Suddenly I heard a voice coming from the table behind us, saying: "Hey, you're going to put my wife's eye out with that umbrella!"

I apologised and moved it away. I turned to his wife, a woman of about thirty years, who was red in the face with fear and stroking her eye that had just escaped harm at the last moment. Five minutes later, we left the café, and the umbrella remained there alone.

AND VIGNETTES

The Bus

The bus makes its way to the city centre carrying the old men who are on their way to coffee houses and the housewives going to market. It carries men seeking a meaning for their existence and a beautiful woman with a charming presence. The bus passes houses from whose balconies no one looks out and the church which is swathed in silence. It passes the park where lovers meet. The woman of charming presence gets off the bus and chooses a bench for herself in the lovers' park. She watches the buses, which stop for a moment at the edge of the park and then carry on as usual to the city centre. The woman spends her day off waiting on the park bench for the man who told her he was seeking a meaning for his existence. She leaves the park in the evening. The man looking for the woman with a charming presence gets off the bus before it stops by the park. He is looking for a meaning for his existence, which seems a mystery to him, an unfathomable mystery in every way.

Performance

The gypsy band plays its tunes in the tree-shaded square. Women leaving the polished offices pause for a moment, then make their way home or go off to mysterious meetings. Men hurry across the square as if barking dogs are chasing at their heels. Tramps with thick beards sit or sleep on the old wooden benches and from time to time boys and girls dance or exchange kisses. A solitary woman listens to the band's tunes for about half an hour and then wanders off aimlessly down the streets, not knowing how to finish her day. A solitary man listens to the band in a somewhat sorrowful fashion. He stays until it finishes playing.

The melodies fade away into the silence and the man gets up and goes off for two or three hours. He comes back to the square with the woman who did not know how to end her day. The band has vanished for some reason or other and the square is empty except for three of the tramps who are snoring, fast asleep, and the band-leader who is staring into space with only a tired musical instrument and bottle of wine in front of him.

A Map

The man strolls through the city streets at a leisurely pace. The map, whose twisting lines he gazes at, leads him to many different places: sometimes it leads him to moments of love; most of the time it leads him to solitude and sorrow. The woman walks through the city streets. The map leads her to specific places. She feels that each one of her steps should be calculated with the utmost precision in order to avoid the risk of exposing herself to disconcerting possibilities.

Rain pours down on the city submerging the streets and squares. The man throws the map into the water's depths. It rises to the surface and floats away. In a moment of exasperation, the woman throws her map into the water's depths and surrenders herself to the map inside her. The man surrenders himself to the map inside him. After five minutes they meet. The man greets the woman with a longing smile as if he has been waiting for her for years, and the woman does the same, as if she has been waiting for him for years. The man takes another step towards the woman but an immense map falls from some-where and blocks the narrow space between them. Nei-ther one can see the other any more, or even reach the other's fingertips.

A Visit

On the last feast which came after the recent massacre, we sat cradling our sorrows in the heavy silence. The martyrs came into the room one by one and didn't greet us. They sat on the chairs, wrapped in shrouds. The bereaved woman came in, steeped in mourning. She poured the bitter coffee from the copper pitcher and steam rose from her gloomy coffee cups. Hands and hearts amongst us trembled. We drank the coffee and softly murmured words of mourning. The martyrs sat there in their shrouds as if the whole affair had nothing to do with them, and then suddenly they disappeared.

Isolation

That man, who lost his leg in a bitter fight between family members over something petty, not worth mentioning, eats one meal a day. He does not leave the house except in the late afternoon, when he goes out on crutches and stands silently in the courtyard, speaking to no one. He stands like a stork, watching the autumn sun until it sets. He goes back to his room with his head bowed and shuts the door behind him. He puts the crutches next to the bed and they go to sleep. He stays awake listening carefully, waiting for someone to knock on his door for some reason or other, any reason.

A Window

That wicked boy wears an earring in his right ear and tells his companions that he wears it to set himself apart from everyone else. He goes out in the neighbourhood bare-chested, showing off in front of the pretty girls and announcing that he has no respect for any of the men in the neighbourhood. In the evening he sits outside the local bar. After the proprietor of the bar has locked up he sits there alone, smoking a cigarette that gives off an unusual smell. He coughs from time to time, and in a raucous voice sings a lewd song to a beautiful woman in the neighbourhood who is married with three children. He sings so that the woman might hear him from the window of her room, not knowing that she moved away from the neighbourhood three weeks ago.

Fragrances

That distant forest now fills the realm of memory. That tender evening comes, bringing all its possibilities with it. Those fragrances that embrace move closer at a stroke, borne on the back of the wind that carries them from one city to another and from one street to another, until they land near the troubled man who smells them cautiously.

There were trees and water, water and violets, a stickiness captivating hearts, gasping breaths and a woman saying "don't go away". Yet the wind, as always, is kind to no one and does not keep the secret. Here it comes, bearing the forest, the evening, the fragrances and the gasping breaths on its back. It enters without asking. The man's troubles grow, one upon the other, as he watches the wind sitting on the chair waiting to be overcome with sleep. It sleeps, or makes some excuse, and then rises up and leaves through the window, bearing the forest and the rest of the secrets on its back.

Eyes

The murderer can spread our blood all over the place, as he likes. He can send us to death one by one, or in groups. He can wash our blood from his hands at some late hour in the evening and then go to his home, which was our home, and sleep. He can wake up a little after midnight to contemplate us as, one by one, we gather in his little bedroom. He cannot remember in which street he shot us and he tosses and turns in his bed, sweating. We sit around him on simple seats made of straw, which by chance we have brought along with us, and continue to stare into his eyes, the whole time saying nothing.

The Room

How pathetic he was, that murderer in his military uniform. How pathetic and ugly he was, looking out from the television screen for the entire world to see, threatening the defenceless town that a large quantity of firebombs would be fired at their houses which were drowning in grief and gloom.

He could have been a well-mannered murderer so that we could have found some excuse for him. He could have been a murderer with a good argument, so that we could have had a little admiration for him. But he was pathetic and ugly. Testimony to this was the child's bedroom, which was ripped apart, his bed, which was burnt, the rabbit, the elephant, the giraffe, the duck and spatters everywhere of his blood. They posed a risk to that ugly murderer who did not have a good argument so that we could have had a little admiration for him.

The Youth

That tender-skinned youth did not stint in giving his blood for us. He understood, by virtue of his good instincts, that we needed clean air and a country, so he did not stint.

It was his right to live so that he could get to know the country's cities, one by one. It was his right to live so that he could go to university and read, at the least, ten thousand books. It was his right to live so that he could have a beautiful wife who would share the worries and joys of the world with him. It was his right to live so that he could live, like everybody else. Yet he understood by virtue of his good instincts that we . . . so he didn't stint. There he is leaving us now, clutching to the last a stone that he was going to hurl at the enemy.

A City

They are discussing a forthcoming play. The writer promises unequivocally that the text, which he will start writing tomorrow evening, will befit a city that has resisted so many invasions. The producer undertakes to raise sufficient funding, even if he has to take out bank loans, to honour the city ruined by an invasion that relied on the latest weapons and the oldest myths. The director says that as of this evening he will start looking for the woman upon whom he will base the leading role. He says, as he contemplates the empty space: "I want her to be a woman who is extremely raunchy and at the same time resolutely defiant so that she might be worthy of the role for a city which invaders have laid to waste, time after time throughout its history. Yet which buried all its invaders and has lived throughout the ages."

Fear

They go down into the deep wadi. They go down with baskets in their hands, and blankets and scraps of cloth tied to old copper containers on their backs, which have been weakened by toil and hardship. They go down watching warily as darkness gathers on the distant horizons. In the houses, to which they will return after many long months, there are women sitting in silence. They have locked the doors, shut the windows firmly and barricaded the paths leading to the bewildering emptiness in their hearts, an emptiness that grows ever bigger in the harsh nights of their loneliness.

Betrayal

The woman, in her black ankle-length dress, stands next to the man in the grey coat. A wild wind rages outside. The windows shake and an incessant whistling comes from them; clouds scud across the sky like people fleeing falling bombs.

Evening steals in through the doors and windows. Without a word, the man takes the woman by the hand and leads her along the dimly lit street which has been left at the wind's mercy. The woman follows him, not knowing where he is leading her but finding pleasure in this. The pleasure stays with her until a few months later, when she goes back to the same street on account of the wind that is beating against the windows and the unsettling evening; and the man appears at the end of the street leading another woman who is laughing in the twilight without a care. Laughing, as if he will never leave her.

AND MORE
VIGNETTES

Silence

She sits in the corner of the room and the heavy silence rises sadly in her heart. She examines everything around her, as is her habit: she looks at the wall, at the pictures of the sons who departed, and in their arms laughing girls in wedding dresses. She does not let her eyes linger there for long, because the girls are sly.

She contemplates the beautiful plants in the corners of the room and high on the wall and feels a desire to weep because the beautiful plants in her room do not speak to her.

She gazes at the bare legs of the chair, whose appearance does not appeal to her. The chair seems to want to surprise her by rushing outside the house and proceeding aimlessly along the roads. She moves warily toward the door, ascertains that it is well locked, then approaches the chair – which now seems like a wicked child who suppresses a laugh – to stop it from escaping again.

She turns her back on it and moves away, suddenly hearing the sound of a body crashing to the floor. She shivers in fear and alarm, then grasps after a moment a petal from the creeping plant which has thrown itself down; it seems that it could not abide all this silence, all this time, so high up on the wall.

Engagement

It is March, with warm rain and gentle sun, and look – it is the delicious, cloudless hour. The girl claims she is going out to gather mushrooms from the spring hillock. The mother does not object, and continues to recite Qur'anic incantations.

He arrives at the appointed time from the opposite direction: a handsome youth, with three goats and a suckling kid rushing in front of him. They sit on the hillock: he spreads his shabby coat under her and picks a bouquet of wild flowers for her in the hope it will make her less shy. They pass the time following a snail which creeps near them with only a shell on its back. They wonder which direction it will take away from them. Then they are seized by a slight restlessness.

There emerges from a distant house the funeral procession of the man who lived for 110 years. The warm rain

pours down anew, hastening the steps of the funeral procession. The snail disappears inside its shell, and the girl,
set afire by the rain, lies on the youth's coat like land that
is thirsty and inviting.

Longing

She knows, since he told her the tale of an absent lover,
that she will lose him one evening. She will search for
him in the house, on the roads, in every place they used
to frequent, without discovering an answer.

He knows that he will miss her one morning and not
be able to search for her because he will be deprived of
the chance to visit the places or cross the distances.

Once, an obscure rumour reached her, and she came
out running like a filly until she arrived at his distant
house, not daring to enter. The house was populated by
silence, and darkness grew on the walls.

Vow

There is a painting on the wall: a glass bottle and a few apple pips; and a song on the cassette: "I yearn for my mother's coffee".★ And outside the rain pecks at the windowpanes.

In front of him is a glass of wine and in his heart a distant country grows – rain washes an ancient wall, wet wooden windows, domes and minarets and crosses; an armoured military car passes in the middle of the street spraying rainwater from under its wheels; church bells ring mournfully – it is Sunday. He comes through a glass door to where he sips Latrun wine and dreams of a cloudless sky and streets where serenity is not troubled by armoured cars.

The rain stops and the image vanishes. He returns his gaze to the silent painting, the song melting away . . . How far away he is from this country! He gulps down the glass of wine in one go and goes out to the street, watching the water flooding like memories. Then he leans on the eucalyptus in his heart and writes on its trunk a vow.

★ This song, from Mahmoud Darwish's poem "Ila Ummi" ["To my mother"] became one of Marcel Khalifah's most popular songs.

Killing

The enemy soldiers halt to check his identity, which does not startle him: in his pocket, a picture of his beloved, and in his house, his mother does not hide anything but sweet potatoes and wheat. At night, she knits a woollen stocking for his little sister in preparation for the cold winter, then goes to bed, dreaming of peace and security.

They lead him away to prison, ripping up the picture of his beloved and trampling it under their feet. They interrogate him and he is tortured for many days: What are you hiding in the house? He says: Nothing. Nothing but sweet potatoes and wheat. What he means by these words is unclear to them.

They turn the house upside down from top to bottom. They find nothing but sweet potatoes and wheat and an unfinished stocking. They do not cease, then, from torturing him: they believe that a person who hides sweet potatoes and wheat is likely also to hide bombs and weapons.

They continue torturing him until he dies. Then they reveal to the public that he died of his own accord and without coercion.

Deprivation

The child who wakes from his sleep in the dark morning is not able to arouse his mother from her deep sleep. He sits there near her on the bed, watching her face, which is motionless like the surface of water.

The child who wakes from his sleep early in the morning is hungry and leans over the side of his mother's chest in order to draw out her breast from the nightgown, but his childish hands fail.

The suckling child starts to cry. People come from all directions and crowd into the house. They wail in the house for some time, then they carry the child's mother to a place that, until now, he does not know of.

Mahmoud Shukair

Funeral

The thin midddle-aged man with the long, ridiculed neck is dead, and believing he lived a clamorous life. He worked playing a tambourine in nightclubs, with forty-seven dancers shaking their hips to its rhythm. Each of them has a story, but no one knows their secrets except for him.

The thin middle-aged man was convinced, as he died, departing in his hut, that the woman dancers would not stay away from the funeral, they would surely strike their cheeks in mourning – cheeks heavily covered with make-up – and feel sorry about his death.

The thin middle-aged man is dead, and the women dancers are absorbed in their afternoon nap, in preparation for a long night of feverish dancing. No one went to his funeral except the cemetery guard, two people who were passing on the road, four more who stopped as a good deed, and a miserable dog with a bobbed tail.

Storm

He only knows that he was bending toward her cheek, in a vague moment, when a storm broke out. The evening was pale, grasping the trees of the road with its dark eyelashes. The world was wrapped in this song against cold wind and clouds; and he does not know why, but as he bent down to pluck a rose from her cheek, a storm exploded suddenly in the air and startled his beloved as if she were a doe, afraid of the vague talking of the gossipy towns.

The Sea

The abundant green country reminds him of another country, a place which he longs for but which remains far away. He stands on the quiet hotel balcony, studying the expanse of the sea awhile and the embracing trees on the adjacent hill. He is provoked by the absolute silence, and goes down to the hotel foyer: no one is there except the elderly clerk, whose eyes are full of a spiritless tranquillity.

He climbs the paths that lead through the trees to the top of the hill, where many sparrows sing happily. A mother sparrow returns with the evening, carrying seeds for her little ones. He doesn't find anyone else strolling on the hill and grief wells up inside him. He amuses himself by looking at the sea. It is far away now and there is a ship slowly penetrating the black darkness, going out into the wide universe. The ship conceals its secrets from him, and his estrangement grows.

He quickly descends the hill and walks along the shore that separates the hotel from the sea. He contemplates the beach umbrellas scattered over the sand: there is nothing that evening except the silent umbrellas and the whispering undulations of the sea, there are no men or women walking on the shore.

He hears soft music coming from the ground floor of the hotel that faces the sea. He hurries toward the source of the music. There is a ballroom, swirling with men and women, some of them swaying in time with their partners on the dance floor, others crowding around the tables. He looks at the women's legs, burnt by the beach sun. He feels that the rhythm of this music, which allows a man and a woman to meet and dance, is nothing less than the happiness of living in a homeland that is not arrested in chains.

He approaches a solitary woman and asks her permission to sit down. She murmurs a word he doesn't catch. A smile comes over him, as he takes it for an invitation to join her, and he pulls the chair backwards before sitting down. A man comes to the table carrying two glasses of beer. The woman reaches for a glass, they toast and then become engrossed in conversation.

He returns the chair to its place and withdraws in silence. He strides away across the sluggish sand, gazing far into the distance. The ships have completely vanished. This oppresses him and increases his awareness of his own loneliness; it merges with the mumbling of the sea so that he realises he is as alone as a child and as sad as a captive country.

Parting

They part, scattering in all directions. The boy walks after his mother slowly, paying no attention to her persistent shouts. His eyes are fastened on the beauty of the rocks and their wonderful formations, which remind him of pictures of different animals.

His mother turns to him and yanks him by his ear in front of everyone in the group. He walks behind her sadly, no longer attracted to the rocks in their varied shapes. A feeling insinuates itself in his heart that there are many frustrations concealing the beauty of this world.

His mother's complaints about how long the road is increase, her booming voice racing along. The boy nears his mother, and takes his little sister's hand. He leads her across winding paths, becoming aware that he is becoming prematurely older. These were his first steps away from his distant homeland, but he did not know the meaning of that until much later.

TALKING
ABOUT WRITING

My journey in writing

It happens that sometimes I pause to look back and consider parts of my journey within writing, and each time I am reassured that I was right to choose to be a writer of short stories rather than of other kinds of literature.

The decisive moment which truly forged my attachment to the short story was linked to the sudden appearance of the Jerusalem magazine *Al-Ufuq al-Jadeed [New Horizon]* in 1961. I got hold of a copy of the first issue and was entertained by the stories it contained. They spoke of some parts of the Palestinian *naqba* – the catastrophe of 1948 – and gripped me with a passion such that I started writing stories full of rhetoric and tradition.

★ ★ ★

It was *New Horizon* that chose to nurture my work and refine my talent, and it took part in the shaping of an entire generation of poets, storytellers and critics. The editor-in-chief was the poet Amin Shanar. He had the important role of paving the difficult way forward for our generation, which profited so much from his patronage. I continued my pursuit of knowledge and learning through my fictional experiments. I finished reading books by Palestinian and Arab writers, and, without pausing, continued to seek what was available in English translation. My relationship with the short story compelled me to read and translate whatever examples of it were given to me in English, and I was able to publish translations of stories by Ernest Hemingway, John Steinbeck and others. I don't deny that I was influenced, too, by the stories of Chekhov and Yusuf Idris. From reading these writers, I became concerned with the search for my own particular voice in the short story form.

My childhood was occupied by the folktale, and since there wasn't a radio in our house until the mid-50s, there was no family pastime for evenings, before bed, other than the telling of folktales, a task undertaken with great seriousness by my mother and one of my uncles, whose rendition of these tales was an art. We would listen with rapt attention as he told us all about the heroes of his folktales – from the greatest to the most evil. These stories coloured our nights with all shades and ranges of colours, but he didn't stop with that. He used to tell his sister, my mother – in a whisper sometimes or out loud at other times – about his adventures with women in distant villages. [. . .] Later, the subject of women would become a major topic in my writing.

And it was these evening gatherings in my grandfather's guesthouse which taught me the art and craft of story-telling and developed my interest in it. The guesthouse was a kind of challenge to me. The conversations that went on there were not open to just anyone, and there were rules for conversing which everyone observed. I was forced to be silent within the walls of the diwan until my adolescent years, so that when the time came for me to break this silence, my shy attempts were ignored.

★ ★ ★

So I found that the thing which produced the most contentment in my soul was to retreat into my own special guesthouse, to build it on paper, and there I could move across its spacious interior without words or conversation. I was the lord and creator, I was responsible for it and in control of it.

Writing was my retaliation against the hegemony of silence. There I sought refuge whenever I came across a need in my soul for confession, or a desire to challenge my grandfather's guesthouse.

★ ★ ★

In the mid-sixties the communist movement attracted my attention. I was interested in its literature that spoke about efforts to help the poor, and for over two years, I joined in a dialogue with them. [. . .] I joined the Communist Party and started to consider myself one of the writers of Socialist Realism. This new experience improved my political awareness and gave me an ability to perceive what was fundamental in reality. But I eventually lost my spontaneity and innocence in perceiving and dealing with the world, due to the mechanical, literal understanding of Marxism during those years. At that time, ideology had become a dominant force in some of my stories, but I realise now I should not have allowed it such a prominent place in my work, since it weakens artistic creation.

By the mid-seventies, I found myself incapable of writing the discursive, traditional type of short story that I had earlier fixed on. The general rhythm of life had changed and my perception of things had become so much more enriched, due to my constant reading, but especially due to my increasing life experience in the areas of exile and diaspora.

Within the Arab literary world, modernism and experimentation in the short story genre had reached almost every corner. I was lucky to be influenced by this movement and to influence it, in return, through my second collection of stories, *The Palestinian Boy*, in which I embarked on this risky and new experimental short story, beginning with a powerful economy of language, as well as a concentration of focus to produce an ultimate simplicity.

What keeps worrying me, all the time, is the sense that writing, to a great extent, is a manipulation with limitations and is not easily manageable. Sometimes the ability to write deserts me (so that I am incapable of writing). I become afflicted by a defeated and exhausted feeling and do not know what to offer to my readers. This desertion, and the struggle to try to write, makes me grumble and complain constantly. This takes up a lot of time and blocks the moment of inspiration. When writer's block ends, however, my doubts vanish.

Hemingway
in Jerusalem

I began reading Ernest Hemingway when I was twenty-two and wished I'd discovered him earlier.

From the very first stories and novels I read I sensed that here was a writer who could captivate his reader. From the beginning I was amazed by his simple, inimitable prose style, flowing sentences that in most instances began with a verb, and his cunning way of disguising himself in the text, presenting himself to the reader as objective and impartial. This way of writing, I believe, made a deep impression on me. That was in the early 1960s at a time when Jerusalem celebrated culture and writers had a role in the city, in complete contrast to today.

I and a group of young men began writing for the Jerusalem-based magazine *New Horizon* [*al-Ufuq al-Jadeed*] that first emerged in 1961. The appearance of the magazine at this time, I believe, played a major role in bringing us into the arena of creative writing, in refining our talents, and in focusing our attention on international literature. Fortunately, there was a fairly lively translation movement in Cairo and Beirut at the time and there were bookshops in Jerusalem that stocked books from the publishing houses in those two cities including, of course, translations of the most important international authors. Critical essays and book reviews published in *New Horizon*, along with the Lebanese *al-Adaab* magazine, played an important role in acquainting us with the books we should read. Thus I came to know the work of Ernest Hemingway, John Steinbeck, Albert Camus, Jean-Paul Sartre, Erskine Caldwell, Colin Wilson and others.

I would head joyfully for the bookshops on Salah al-Din Street and Al-Zahra Street to see what new books had arrived. I was always buying books: poetry collections, volumes of stories, novels, as were my writer friends, who later became known as the '*New Horizon* generation'. We would buy the books from Cairo and Beirut, read and discuss them, and sometimes even venture to write something about them. During these years, as an aspiring writer only just finding his feet, I began to read in English. I would go to the American Information Centre, situated on one of the side streets off Sharia Salah al-Din, and borrow a book in Arabic and English. I became so drawn to both Hemingway and Steinbeck that I undertook to translate their stories from English into Arabic. My translations of Hemingway's "Soldier's Home" and Steinbeck's "The Snake" were published in *New Horizon*.

Hemingway made a huge impression on us, not only in the realm of literature but also in our daily lives. We began to frequent coffee shops in such a manner that heads would be turned, imitating Hemingway who spent all his time in cafés in the cities he visited. (When I was in Madrid in 1988 I just had to visit the café where Hemingway used to sit and went there with one of my Spanish friends. We sat together, remembering Hemingway and his mad love of bull-fighting and friendships with the sport's heroes).

We had our favourite coffee shops in Salah al-Din Street and Al-Zahra Street, as well as in the old city. We loved sitting in coffee shops and it supplied us with new material for our stories. Never would we walk those city streets without books under our arms as evidence that we were intellectuals soon to make our mark on the world of literature.

Hemingway's novels and short stories broadened my horizons and enriched my soul in no small way. As I walked the streets, climbed the steps of buildings, rode buses, and studied the people, the buildings and everything else around me I felt I was in the world of a novel. I pictured myself as a literary hero just stepped out of a book, walking the streets and sitting in cafés with characters from Hemingway's novels and short stories. They appeared pleasant and friendly as they strove, prescribed by destiny, for a better life, though their efforts almost always ended in failure.

When I read *A Farewell to Arms* (1929) I was thrilled by Hemingway's deployment of hot weather in the love story that explodes between the wounded soldier and nurse looking after him in hospital. Oh, how the scenes set in the pouring rain delighted me! When I read Hemingway's short stories the unpretentious elegance of their titles caught my attention, for example "A Clean, Well-Lighted Place" (1933), "Old Man at the Bridge" (1938) and so on. I was also attracted to his turn of phrase and flowing prose that used delicate allusions to captivate the reader and encourage him to play an active role in reshaping the work of art. Hemingway does not tell the reader everything. Rather, as critics, including the famous American Carlos Baker, have noted, he touches only the tip of the iceberg and leaves the rest buried deep below the ocean's surface. By leaving his stories open to interpretation in this way Hemingway lends his stories a lasting and universal significance.

In the early 1960s I was searching for answers to the many questions to do with existence, society, life and mankind that had dogged me for years. I began to incline towards the Left as I learned more and more about it in Hemingway's writings. I loved his novel *For Whom the Bell Tolls* (1940) which portrays his sympathy for the Spanish people in their fight against fascism. Hemingway's predilection for secularism and support of socialism and its struggle against fascism was, for me, good reason to pursue my interest in this American philanthropist's work. This was reinforced when I read *The Old Man and The Sea* where I saw the struggle of the old man Santiago, the novel's hero, with the hungry sharks in the rough sea as a symbol for the struggle against evils powers wherever they are. The way Santiago 's fishing expedition ends in no way diminished the value of the novel and its underlying themes and messages. My writer friends and I worked hard at the time to squeeze more meaning out of this great humanist novel and it was no surprise that we reached the conclusion that the novel – in its portrayal of Santiago's long and exhausting fishing trip where his only reward is the carcass of a giant fish which he throws on to the shore as he walks off to get some well-deserved rest – ultimately represents the common struggle of mankind. We saw the carcass as a metaphor for all that is left behind from man's journey through life.

That was in the first half of the 1960s. Then came the June war of 1967 and the beginning of Israel's occupation of the West Bank, Gaza Strip and East Jerusalem. The Palestinian people thus suffered a Nakba, a setback. similar to that of 1948; and the occupation had a hugely damaging effect on intellectual activity in Jerusalem and the rest of the Occupied Territories. The writing community was thrown into disarray, some of its members were arrested, others were forced into exile by the Israeli occupation, while the rest fell silent and stopped writing. *New Horizon* ceased to exist and daily newspapers disappeared until a year into the occupation. The bookshops we used to buy books from were no longer able to import new books because of the occupation policy that imposed a blockade on people. The result was that the cultural scene dwindled and entered a period of stagnation that lasted several years.

I could not continue with Hemingway until I was myself exiled from the homeland eight years into the war. The occupation authorities exiled me to Lebanon; there, in Beirut, and afterwards in Amman, I was once again able to read Hemingway. The last book I read was *A Moveable Feast* (1964), which might be regarded as a personal journey of sorts or short story, though not in the strict meaning of the word. I observed that Hemingway was still true to his delicate allusion and inimitable simple prose style, never affected or laborious. I also observed Hemingway's tendency to run down people he had known in his work, perhaps from hatred or jealousy, perhaps because of his own bad mood and egoitism, which were characteristics I had not recognised in my favourite writer during the early years when I was naïve and eagerly seeking perfection!

When I read Paul Johnson's book *The Intellectuals* I discovered things about Hemingway I hadn't known before, for example, his deep loathing of his mother, his authoritarian approach to his four wives, his tendency to exaggerate and lie, his jealousy of other writers' successes and rancour towards them (with the exception of the poet Ezra Pound who remained in Hemingway's affection because of the latter's high morality and concern for other writers).

Perhaps the facts are true, perhaps some are true and others false. This doesn't interest me, particularly as that is all in the past! What interests me is that Hemingway's novels and short stories were, and still are, able to enrich human existence with noble values and hidden pleasure. This is why Hemingway has had a positive influence on both my soul and my writing. I always remember him with affection and respect. I recognise him as my superior and hold him in high estimation.

The Translators

Issa J. Boullata is a Palestinian writer, literary critic and translator. He is formerly Professor of Arabic Literature at McGill University, Montreal, Canada. He is the author of several works of literary criticism, also a novel in Arabic (1998). His translations include Jabra Ibrahim Jabra's memoirs *Princesses' Street* (2005) and *The First Well* (1995), Mohamed Berrada's *The Game of Forgetting* (1986), Emily Nasrallah's *Flight Against Time* (1997), and Ghada Samman's *The Square Moon* (1998). He is a contributing editor of *Banipal*.

Elizabeth Whitehouse graduated in Arabic from St. Andrews University, Scotland, and obtained an MA from SOAS, London University. She lives and works in France.

Elizabeth Winslow is a fiction writer and a graduate of the Iowa Writers' Workshop, USA. Her translations include Dunya Mikhail's *The War Works Hard* (New Directions, 2005), which won the American PEN prize for translation and was short-listed for the Griffin International Poetry Prize 2006. Some of her translated poems have been published in *Modern Poetry in Translation*, *Poetry International*, *Words Without Borders*, *Circumference* and *World Literature Today*.

Christina Phillips has a PhD in Modern Arabic Literature from SOAS, University of London, and has translated a number of works from Arabic, most recently Naguib Mahfouz's *Hadith al-Sabah wa'l-Masa* (*Morning and Evening Talk*, AUC Press, 2007). She is presently pursuing postdoctoral research into religion in modern Arabic literature.

Acknowledgements

Shakira's Picture is the title story of the author's short story collection *Surat Shakira [Shakira's Picture]*, Al-Muassassa al-Arabiyah, Beirut/Amman, 2003, first published in English translation in *Banipal*, No 20, Spring 2004. **Ronaldo's Seat** and the title story **My Cousin Condoleezza** were translated especially for this volume from the author's collection *Ebnat Khalati Kondouliza [Daughter of my Aunt Condoleezza]*, Al-Muassassa al-Arabiyah, Beirut/Amman 2004. **Mordechai's Moustache and his Wife's Cats** was published online at www.kikah.com and first published in English translation in *Banipal* No 20, Spring 2004. The stories grouped under VIGNETTES were translated especially for this collection from the author's collection *Ihtimalat Tafifa [Small Probabilities]*, Al-Muassassa al-Arabiyah, Beirut /Amman 2006. The stories grouped under AND VIGNETTES were published in their original Arabic in the monthly cultural magazine *Amman*, No 84, June 2002, Amman, Jordan, and the cultural magazine founded by Emile Habiby, *Masharef*, No 17, Summer 2002, Haifa, Israel. They were first published in English translation in *Banipal* No 15/16, Autumn 2002/Spring 2003. The stories grouped under AND MORE VIGNETTES are translated from the author's collection *Tuqoos lil Mara'ah al-Shaqiyya [Rites for a Miserable Woman]* and first published in *Banipal* No 7, Spring 2000.

My Journey in Writing is an edited transcript of a speech given by the author in Amman, Jordan, first published in English translation in *Banipal* No 7, Spring 2000. **Hemingway in Jerusalem** was written especially for the regular feature in *Banipal* magazine, LITERARY INFLUENCES, and first published in *Banipal* No 20, Summer 2004.

Other fiction titles from Banipal Books

*Order online from www.banipal.co.uk
or from your local bookshop*

A Retired Gentleman and other stories *by Issa J. Boullata*
ISBN 978-0-9549666-6-9 2007   pbk 120pp £7.99
A rich medley of tales about emigrants to Canada and the US from
Palestine, Lebanon, Egypt and Syria that will continue resonating long after
the book is put down.

The Myrtle Tree *by Jad el Hage*
ISBN 978-0-9549666-4-5 2007   pbk 288pp £9.99
"Better than any political analysis, this remarkable novel, set in a Lebanese
mountain village, conveys with razor-sharp accuracy the sights, sounds, tastes
and tragic dilemmas of Lebanon's fratricidal civil war." **Patrick Seale**

Unbuttoning the Violin *– translated from Arabic and French*
ISBN 978-0-9549666-2-1 2006   pbk 128pp £3.95
Celebrating the UK tour, Banipal Live 2006, a paperback volume of selected
works by poets Joumana Haddad from Lebanon and Abed Ismael from Syria, and
fiction writers Mansoura Ez-Eldin from Egypt and Ala Hlehel from Palestine

An Iraqi in Paris *by Samuel Shimon, translated from Arabic*
ISBN 978-0-9549666-0-7 2005 pbk 252pp £11.99
Long-listed for the 2007 IMPAC Prize. "It's an Arabic answer to Miller's *Tropic of
Cancer* – occasionally shocking, always witty and humane. Also included is his
delightful memoir of an Iraqi childhood." **Boyd Tonkin,** The Independent

Sardines and Oranges, short stories from North Africa
by 21 Arab authors, translated from Arabic and French
ISBN 978-0-9549666-1-4 2005   pbk 222pp £8.99
Tayeb Salih, Mohamed Choukri, Gamal el-Ghitani and Mohammed Dib are joined
by other leading and newly emerging North African authors in this unique
collaboration of the London Borough of Hammersmith and Fulham with Banipal
Books

Printed in the United Kingdom
by Lightning Source UK Ltd.
123472UK00001B/1-120/A